Breaking Chains

Shattering cycles, Reclaiming Power

Preface

The title of this book, *Breaking Chains*, was inspired by a powerful and transformative prophecy delivered to me during a conference. In that sacred moment, those confirmed words resonated deeply within me, unveiling a divine assignment to break the generational patterns and cycles that had long bound my family, particularly the women.

The prophecy was more than a message—it was a divine mandate. It was a call to step into the role that God had predestined for me, a confirmation that the chains of the past were broken and that a new legacy of freedom, healing, and God's blessings are established for future generations.

This book reflects that journey. It serves as a guide for anyone who feels called to break free from cycles that have held them back. Through personal experiences, biblical insights, and the wisdom imparted by the Holy Spirit, my hope is to empower you to embrace your God-given authority to bring transformation to your life, your family, and beyond.

As you read, may you be inspired to seek the Lord's guidance, find the strength to confront the challenges before you, and walk boldly in the victory already secured through Christ. The journey may not be easy, but with God's grace, the cycles can be broken, and a new chapter can begin.

Table of Contents

Introduction

The notion that everyone deserves to experience a good life is a comforting sentiment, yet life is far from simple or straightforward. It is a journey—unpredictable and challenging—much like navigating a car through the darkness, with only the headlights illuminating a narrow stretch of the road ahead. We can see only what lies immediately before us, while the past gradually fades into distant memory—a collection of moments we cannot physically revisit, no matter how vivid they remain in our minds.

As we move forward, our lives become a rich tapestry of stories and histories, each thread contributing to the larger narrative of who we are and where we come from. These personal and collective narratives hold valuable lessons, not just for ourselves but for others, offering a window into our shared human experience.

Embedded within these stories and histories are cycles and patterns that, to the keen observer, reveal themselves over time. These cycles often span multiple generations, silently shaping behaviors, beliefs, and life choices. It takes a curious mind and a courageous heart to delve into the depths of these generational patterns, curses, and cycles. Recognizing these patterns is no task for the faint-hearted, and the challenge of confronting and breaking them is even more formidable.

Many families, whether knowingly or unknowingly, continue to perpetuate the same cycles across generations—cycles that inhibit growth and bind them to outdated and often harmful ways of thinking and living.

Breaking free from these deeply ingrained patterns requires much more than awareness. It demands profound curiosity to explore the hidden roots of these cycles, revelation to understand their impact, and courage to face them head-on. It requires education to equip oneself with the knowledge to dismantle these patterns, wisdom to apply that knowledge effectively, and, above all, the guidance of the Spirit of God to navigate this intricate and often painful process.

Within the pages of this book, you will encounter true personal stories and profound insights that illuminate the complex journey of breaking generational barriers, curses, cycles, and patterns. These stories are more than mere anecdotes; they are keys to unlocking the chains that may have bound you and your family for generations. By understanding the forces at play, you will be empowered to forge a new path—one that is not only free from the constraints of the past but also brimming with possibilities for the future.

This journey is not just about overcoming the challenges of the past; it is about creating a legacy of positive change. A legacy that will resonate not only in your life but in the lives of those around you and the generations to come. As you embark on this journey, may you find the strength, wisdom, and divine guidance to break free from the chains

that have held you back and step confidently into a future
filled with hope and potential.

CHAPTER I

How Do You Know You Are the Chosen One?

It is only by grace that one can be the chosen one to break generational chains. While it may be clear to you what the issues and patterns are, do not be surprised if other family members remain oblivious to these issues. Do not force your revelation on them. Instead, pray and intercede for them. Be gentle and patient.

Most often, the chosen one is the most misunderstood or even the most disliked member of the family. Remember, people often turn on those who come to save them. Consider the story of Moses in the Bible. He was chosen and sent to free the Jews, yet his journey was fraught with rejection and misunderstanding. Free people, whether spiritually or physically, perceive things differently from those who are enslaved.

When Moses saw an Egyptian master mistreating a Jew, he acted out of passion and killed the master. Later, when he saw two Jews fighting, he lovingly advised them to stop. Instead of heeding his advice, they threatened to expose him. This story illustrates how fragile and isolating the position of the chosen one can be.

Breaking generational curses is a process that requires patience and grace. It also requires cultivating forgiveness. Understand that your efforts are not just for you—they will benefit your children and future generations, including nieces, nephews, and cousins. They will witness that you did not settle and see what freedom from these cycles looks like. From there, they can learn healthy patterns from you, fostering a new and positive legacy.

Being the chosen one means embracing a difficult yet rewarding journey. Here are some key points I have learned from my personal experience:

1. **Awareness and Clarity** Recognize the patterns and issues that need to be broken. This awareness is a gift that not everyone in your family may have.
2. **Patience and Intercession** Pray and intercede for your family members who may not see what you see. Avoid forcing your understanding upon them.
3. **Facing Resistance** Understand that being chosen often means facing resistance and even hostility from those you are trying to help. You might be viewed as the black sheep of the family. This is a common experience for those called to break cycles and bring about change.
4. **The Example of Moses** Like Moses, your passion and actions may not always be understood or appreciated. Be prepared for misunderstandings and opposition, but remain steadfast in your mission.
5. **Cultivate Forgiveness** Forgive those who do not understand your mission or resist the changes you are trying to bring. Forgiveness is crucial for your peace and the success of your mission.

6. **Focus on Future Generations** Your efforts will pave the way for future generations to live free from the patterns you are breaking. They will learn from your example and create healthier cycles.
7. **Embrace the Process** Breaking generational curses is a process. It requires time, patience, and perseverance.

By embracing your role and following these principles, you can break generational cycles and set a new, positive trajectory for your family. Your efforts will not be in vain, and future generations will thank you for the freedom and clarity you have brought into their lives.

Observing My Family Patterns

I was fortunate to be raised in a family adorned with beauty, courage, and cultivated wisdom—a family filled with visionary women whose dedication to hard work was unwavering. Growing up amidst such inspiring figures was nothing short of a joyous blessing. Witnessing my sisters embark on their journeys of marriage and motherhood, raising beautiful children of their own, only added to the richness of my upbringing.

As the 13th child and youngest daughter among 13 siblings, I was born into a family where the bond between my parents formed the cornerstone of a truly remarkable household. My mother, a woman of grace and resilience, epitomized beauty and diligence. She exuded wisdom and strength as a devoted wife and displayed unparalleled nurturing and selflessness as a mother. Her presence infused our home with warmth and stability, creating an environment where love and respect thrived.

My father, a pillar of strength and integrity, complemented my mother's unwavering devotion with his steadfast commitment to our family. Together, they instilled in me the values of hard work, perseverance, and faith, laying the foundation for the strong sense of unity and purpose that defined our family dynamic.

Despite being the youngest among my siblings, I never felt overshadowed or overlooked. On the contrary, my parents' boundless love and unwavering support made me feel cherished and valued. This ignited within me a sense of purpose and determination to live up to their expectations.

As I reflect on my upbringing, I am filled with gratitude for the countless blessings bestowed upon me by my family. Their love, guidance, and unwavering faith have shaped me into the person I am today, instilling in me the values of resilience, compassion, and steadfast faith that continue to guide me on my journey through life.

From an early age, my parents instilled in me a deep reverence for God, teaching me the scriptures and the importance of prayer. My father, in particular, imparted invaluable lessons on faith, emphasizing the significance of unwavering belief in the divine. Together, we journeyed through the pages of the Bible, from Genesis to Revelation, immersing ourselves in its teachings twice over.

Attention Received from Parents

Being the youngest child came with its privileges, yet it also bred envy and resentment among my siblings. My parents' special attention toward me, fueled by their desire for my success, set me apart. I understood their aspirations and endeavored to fulfill them with determination. However, my journey was not without its trials.

Growing up, I was accustomed to the privileges of being the youngest, but I could not ignore the envy and resentment it sometimes stirred among my siblings. My parents, especially my father, played a significant role in shaping my spiritual foundation. Their teachings on scripture and the importance of prayer instilled in me a deep reverence for God from an early age.

Their special attention, driven by their hopes for my success, often made me feel set apart. I understood their expectations and I strove to meet them with unwavering determination. Yet, the path was far from smooth.

As I navigated through life, I encountered trials that tested my faith and resolve. Moments of doubt and uncertainty arose, where I questioned the path laid out before me. Yet, through it all, the lessons instilled by my parents, particularly my father, served as guiding lights in the darkness.

His emphasis on the importance of faith and maintaining an unwavering belief in the divine became my anchor during life's stormy seas. I learned to lean on prayer as a source of strength and solace, seeking guidance and wisdom in times of need.

Despite the challenges and setbacks, I remained steadfast in my faith, trusting in a higher power to guide me through life's twists and turns. My upbringing imbued me with resilience and perseverance—qualities that have helped me weather the storms and emerge stronger on the other side.

In retrospect, I am deeply grateful for the foundation laid by my parents, whose love and guidance shaped me into the person I am today. Their teachings continue to resonate within me, serving as a constant reminder of the importance of faith, perseverance, and unwavering belief in the divine.

Innocent Observations of My Childhood

At every turn of my journey, I found myself navigating a landscape marked by both profound love and intense animosity. In the structured environment of school, where learning should have been the primary focus, I experienced a stark contrast in treatment. Teachers, recognizing my academic prowess and exemplary behavior, often bestowed gifts upon me, positioned me at the forefront of the classroom, and publicly lauded my achievements. Their admiration was palpable, yet it came with its own set of challenges.

While I basked in the glow of their praise, I could not ignore the undercurrent of envy and disdain emanating from some of my peers. The dichotomy between admiration from educators and hostility from fellow students disrupted my equilibrium, casting shadows of doubt and insecurity over my happiness.

The disparity in treatment was glaring. While my teachers celebrated my intellect, diligence, and decorum, I found myself grappling with the weight of resentment and negativity from certain classmates. Although I understood that my teachers' admiration stemmed from genuine recognition of my efforts and abilities, the piercing disdain from my peers often overshadowed any joy I might have derived from academic success.

This internal conflict became a recurring theme in my life—a constant tug-of-war between validation from authority figures and rejection from my peers. It was a struggle that began in my formative years and continued to cast its shadow over my journey, shaping my experiences as I moved through the corridors of education and life in general.

The discordant symphony of love and animosity shaped my perception of self-worth and belonging. I found myself constantly seeking validation from external sources, yearning for acceptance and approval amidst a sea of disapproval. It was a battle fought not only in the classrooms but also within the recesses of my own mind.

Yet, amidst the turmoil, there were moments of clarity. I began to realize that my worth was not contingent upon the opinions of others, whether they were teachers or peers. My value lay in the essence of who I was—in my strengths, weaknesses, and inherent worth as a human being.

Over time, I learned to silence the cacophony of external voices and embrace the melody of my own truth. I discovered that true happiness and fulfillment came from within, from accepting and loving myself unconditionally, flaws and all.

While the journey was fraught with challenges and setbacks, it was also marked by moments of growth and self-discovery. I emerged from the crucible of adversity stronger and more resilient, armed with the knowledge that my worth was not defined by the perceptions of others but by an unwavering belief in my own worthiness.

CHAPTER II

Recognizing A Family Pattern Early On Is Crucial

Recognizing family patterns involves observation, reflection, and awareness of recurring behaviors, dynamics, and interactions within the family unit.

Pay attention to how family members communicate, handle conflicts, and express emotions. Notice recurring themes or dynamics in conversations and interactions.

Consider past events, experiences, and relationships within the family. Look for common themes or patterns that may have influenced the family's dynamics and behaviors over time.

Observe whether certain family members consistently take on specific roles within the family (e.g., caretaker, mediator, troublemaker). Recognize how these roles contribute to the overall family dynamics.

Be mindful of recurring behaviors or responses that occur in various situations. These behaviors may have been passed down through generations or learned from family members.

Understand the values, beliefs, and traditions that shape your family's identity. Reflect on how these factors influence family dynamics and interactions.

Discuss your observations and insights with other family members or trusted individuals outside the family, such as spiritual mentors or counselors. Their perspectives may provide valuable insights and help validate your observations.

Attention

If family patterns are causing significant distress or dysfunction, seeking support from various sources can be highly beneficial. Pastors, therapists, counselors, and prophetic ministries each offer unique perspectives and resources to address family issues.

Therapists and counselors provide guidance, facilitate communication, and help identify constructive solutions based on psychological principles. In contrast, a prophet or prophetic ministry may offer spiritual insights and foresights, providing a perspective rooted in faith. They often offer prayers or spiritual interventions to address underlying issues and break bondages.

When dealing with complex family dynamics, it is important to consider seeking help from multiple sources if needed. Each resource can contribute uniquely to understanding and resolving family challenges.

By actively observing, reflecting, and seeking insight into your family dynamics, you can cultivate a deeper understanding of recurring patterns and their influence on your life. This awareness forms the foundation for addressing and transforming unhealthy or dysfunctional patterns, leading to a healthier and more harmonious version of yourself.

Similarity to Joseph's Story

Growing up, my father ensured that I was well-acquainted with the biblical tale of Joseph—a story of resilience, forgiveness, and divine providence. He praised my thirst for academic excellence and my disciplined approach to life, instilling in me a sense of purpose and destiny from a young age.

As the youngest child in the family, I often found myself at the center of attention, receiving a level of nurturing and guidance that set me apart from my siblings. While this attention should have been a source of joy, it instead fostered a sense of isolation and difference within me. Recognizing the unique position, I held within the family dynamic, my father consistently reminded me not to fear but to trust in God's plan for my life.

In his eyes, I was destined for greatness—meant to rise above any challenge or adversity that crossed my path. He believed fervently that one day, I would be the one to save my family, leading them out of their struggles and into a brighter future.

Though life was good at the time, thanks to my parents' hard work and success, it was a sobering realization that when my father's last day on this earth arrived, his absence would weigh heavily on my siblings and me. Together with our mother, he had been the cornerstone of our family's financial stability and the driving force behind our collective well-being.

In light of this, my father did not want me to succumb to fear or be cowed by potential resentment or envy from my siblings. Instead, he encouraged me to stand firm in my faith and convictions, holding onto the values that define me and guide my actions.

Moreover, he harbored concerns that most of my siblings might not carry forward his legacy of hard work, providence, and self-sufficiency. He recognized the importance of these traits in shaping our family's success and stability, and he hoped that I would continue to uphold and champion these principles, even in his absence.

His words remain a poignant reminder of the responsibility that lies upon my shoulders—to honor his legacy, embody the values he held dear, and navigate the challenges of life with resilience and determination.

As I reflect on his wisdom and guidance, I am reminded of the importance of staying true to myself, remaining steadfast in the face of adversity, and striving to live a life that honors his memory and upholds the principles he cherished.

The tension within the family was palpable, fueled by the disparity in treatment between myself and my siblings. Their feelings of resentment were not born out of anything I had done, but rather from the attention, love, and hope our parents showered upon me as the youngest. This created a rift—a sense of injustice they struggled to reconcile.

In their eyes, I was the favored one, the golden child who could do no wrong. They seized every opportunity to express their resentment, accusing and shaming me in an effort to hurt our parents and expose what they perceived as favoritism. It became a painful cycle of accusation and recrimination, driven by feelings of betrayal and abandonment.

Yet, through it all, my parents remained steadfast in their support of me. Unlike my siblings, who often faced stricter disciplinary measures for their transgressions, I was shielded from the full force of their wrath. They stood by me, unwavering in their belief in my potential and my destiny.

Looking back, I recognize the sacrifices my parents made and the lengths they went to in order to protect and nurture me. Their love was both a blessing and a burden—a source of strength and contention within the family unit. Yet, through their unwavering faith and steadfast devotion, they instilled in me a sense of purpose and resilience that would carry me through the storms of life.

The echoes of Joseph's story resonate deeply within my own life, as I have encountered a pattern of accusations and shame that seems to follow me relentlessly. The story of Joseph and Potiphar's wife presents a parallel complexity, highlighting the interplay between love and hate that mirrors the dynamics within Joseph's own family. Potiphar, the master of the house, held Joseph in high regard, recognizing his integrity and talents. However, this admiration was overshadowed by the false accusation of rape leveled against Joseph by Potiphar's wife (Genesis 39).

The jealousy and animosity harbored by Joseph's siblings toward him stand in stark contrast to the deep love and affection their father, Jacob, held for him. This dichotomy created tension within their family unit, as conflicting emotions threatened to tear them apart. Much like Potiphar's conflicted feelings toward Joseph, Jacob grappled with the complexities of parental love in the face of sibling rivalry and betrayal.

Yet, much like Joseph, I have found solace in the unwavering presence of God, who has continually seen me through the darkest times. Despite others' attempts to tarnish my reputation and bring shame into my life, God's steadfast love and guidance have remained my constant companions.

Struggling to Embrace My Identity

Throughout my life, I have often found myself walking on eggshells, afraid to fully embrace my true self for fear of inviting further accusations and scorn. This perpetual vigilance mirrors the dynamics I experienced with my siblings, where my mere existence seemed to threaten the success and happiness of others. Like Joseph, I have felt marginalized and misunderstood, struggling to find my place in a world that often seeks to diminish my light—even as I excelled in every endeavor.

This reality weighed heavily on my parents, who watched with a mixture of sadness and helplessness as their youngest child grappled with the burden of being the family's star. Unbeknownst to them, they were witnessing the unfolding of a spiritual battle, where I, chosen by God to break generational curses and patterns, stood at the forefront. Though they may not have fully comprehended the magnitude of the struggle, their love and support remained unwavering, serving as beacons of hope in the midst of darkness.

Despite the enemy's relentless efforts to dim my light and undermine my worth, God's plan for my life remains steadfast and unshakable. Just as He made a way for Joseph in the midst of adversity, I am confident that He will continue to guide me and lead me to victory every time.

In the face of accusations and shame, I choose to stand firm in my identity as a child of God, knowing that His love and grace are more than sufficient to sustain me. Though the journey may be fraught with challenges, I walk forward in faith, confident that God's purpose for my life will ultimately prevail.

As the years passed, I found myself growing increasingly distant from my siblings. The constant barrage of negativity and resentment became too much to bear, and I reached a point where I simply couldn't handle it any longer. Despite my earnest desire to be a source of blessing and positivity in their lives, they continued to harbor ill will toward me. It seemed that every success or joyous occasion in my life was met with their worst nightmares coming true.

Much like Joseph's siblings, the dynamics within my own family were complex. Not all of my siblings harbored the same level of animosity toward me. Some remained neutral, indifferent to the tension that permeated our relationships. Others, however, seemed to take pleasure in my misfortunes, actively seeking to undermine my happiness and success. Their actions were fueled by jealousy and resentment, leaving me increasingly isolated within my own family circle.

In this narrative, we witness the intricacies of human relationships, where love and hate coexist in a delicate balance. Potiphar's genuine affection for Joseph is tainted by the betrayal of trust, as he is forced to confront the devastating accusation against his favored servant. Similarly, within Joseph's own family, there exists a complex interplay of emotions, where love and resentment vie for dominance. The story of myself, my siblings, and my parents mirrored this complexity.

In an effort to escape the constant outbursts of negativity and hostility, I sought solace in creating my own metaphorical Egypt—a place of refuge where I could find peace away from the toxicity of familial strife. It became a sanctuary of sorts, a space where I could retreat and regroup, shielding myself from the emotional turmoil that threatened to engulf me.

In this sanctuary, I found solace in the arms of friends and loved ones who offered unwavering support and understanding. Their presence provided a sense of belonging and acceptance that was sorely lacking within my own family dynamic. Together, we forged bonds of friendship and camaraderie that became a lifeline amidst the stormy seas of family discord.

Though the rift within my family remained, I refused to allow it to define me or dictate my destiny. I remained steadfast in my resolve to live a life guided by principles of love, forgiveness, and compassion. While the wounds inflicted by familial strife run deep, I remain hopeful that one-day reconciliation and healing will pave the way for a brighter future.

In the meantime, I continue to seek refuge in my own Egypt, drawing strength from the love and support of those who truly value and cherish me for who I am. Though the journey may be fraught with challenges, I am confident that God's grace will see me through, guiding me toward a future filled with hope and possibility.

CHAPTER III

How to Escape Family Toxicity?

Escaping family toxicity with a spiritual perspective involves integrating your faith and beliefs into your approach to healing and finding peace.

Spend time in prayer and meditation, seeking guidance, strength, and peace from a higher power. Connect with your spirituality to find solace and clarity amidst the chaos of family toxicity. As Matthew 11:28 reminds us: "Come to me, all you who are weary and burdened, and I will give you rest."

Trust in divine guidance to lead you toward healthier relationships and environments. Listen to your intuition and discern the path that aligns with your spiritual values and beliefs.

Practice forgiveness, both for yourself and for those who have caused you pain. Release resentment and bitterness through prayer and meditation, allowing divine love and grace to heal your heart. As Luke 6:37 says, "Forgive, and you will be forgiven." Through these intertwined narratives, we are confronted with the universal themes of love, betrayal, and redemption. The story of Joseph serves as a poignant reminder of the intricacies of human relationships and the enduring power of forgiveness and grace. Despite the trials and tribulations that beset him, Joseph ultimately emerges as a symbol of resilience and hope, a testament to the transformative power of love in the face of adversity.

Establish spiritual boundaries to protect your energy and well-being. Avoid seeking validation from difficult people, and instead, surround yourself with positive influences and environments that nurture your soul and uplift your spirit. Psalms 1:1 advises: "Blessed is the man who walks not in the counsel of the ungodly, nor stands in the way of sinners, nor sits in the seat of the scornful."

Engage in spiritual practices such as attending church services, participating in retreats or gatherings, and studying sacred texts like the Bible or other Godly books. Find inspiration and guidance from spiritual leaders and teachings that nourish your faith.

Cultivate an attitude of gratitude by focusing on the blessings and lessons that arise from challenging experiences. Give thanks to the Almighty, trusting that even amidst toxicity, there are opportunities for growth and transformation.

Seek support and fellowship from a spiritual community or congregation where you feel accepted, understood, and supported. Surround yourself with like-minded individuals who share your faith and values.

Surrender control and trust in God to guide and protect you on your journey. Let go of the need to fix or change others, and instead, focus on your own spiritual growth and evolution.

Remember that escaping the generational patterns of toxicity with a spiritual perspective is a journey of healing and transformation. Trust in the power of divine love and grace to guide you toward inner peace, healing, and wholeness.

My Aunt Norzie Life's Story

As a child, I admired my aunt—my father's sister—with a sense of wonder and fascination. She possessed a natural beauty that seemed to radiate from within. Her tall, slim figure was reminiscent of a model gracing the pages of a magazine. With a flat belly and an air of grace, she exuded an elegance that captivated everyone who crossed her path.

Her smile, framed by beautiful teeth, lit up her face with warmth and sincerity, endearing her to everyone around her. Her skin, clear and light, seemed to glow with an ethereal radiance, adding to her charm and allure.

Yet, despite her outward beauty and magnetic presence, it was her quiet strength and resilience that truly defined her character. She lived with my grandmother, never marrying or having children of her own, yet she embraced her role with a sense of grace and acceptance that spoke volumes about her inner strength.

I never heard her complain or lament her circumstances. Instead, she immersed herself in her work and devoted herself wholeheartedly to caring for her aging mother, selflessly putting her mother's needs above her own. It was as if she had accepted her fate with quiet resignation, finding fulfillment and purpose in the simple act of serving others.

As I watched her navigate life's challenges with grace and dignity, I couldn't help but admire her resilience and unwavering devotion to her family. She may not have had the conventional trappings of success or the outward markers of achievement, but her inner beauty and strength of character were far more precious and enduring.

In her quiet way, she taught me valuable lessons about resilience, sacrifice, and the true meaning of unconditional love. Though she may never grace the pages of a magazine or walk the runway of a fashion show, to those who knew her, she was nothing short of extraordinary.

My Curiosity About My Aunt Norzie

As I grew older, my curiosity about my aunt Norzie's life deepened, fueled by a sense of unease and a nagging feeling that something was amiss. It seemed inconceivable to me that such a beautiful and capable woman could go through life without ever marrying or even having a boyfriend, especially in a culture where marriage and family were highly valued.

While my parents seemed content to accept her situation without question, I could not shake the feeling that there was more to the story than met the eye. Despite their reassurances that everything was fine, my curiosity only grew, driving me to seek answers and uncover the truth.

With determination in my heart, I embarked on a quest to unravel the mystery of my aunt's solitary existence. I began to ask questions, probing gently into her past and piecing together fragments of information from family conversations and memories.

However, the more I searched for answers, the more elusive they became. My aunt remained tight-lipped about her personal life, deflecting questions with a smile or vague responses that revealed nothing of substance. It was as if she were guarding a closely held secret—one she was unwilling or unable to share with us.

Despite the roadblocks and dead ends, I encountered along the way, I refused to give up hope. Deep down, I knew there was a reason behind my aunt's solitary existence—a hidden truth waiting to be unearthed.

More of My Aunt Norzie's Story

As I delved deeper into the recesses of my aunt's past, I remained determined to uncover the truth, no matter where the journey might lead. I knew that only by confronting the shadows of the past could I hope to shed light on the mystery that had haunted me for so long.

Listening intently to my mother's recounting of my aunt Norzie's life story, I felt a mixture of surprise and intrigue wash over me. There was clearly more to my aunt's solitary existence than I had imagined, and I hung onto my mother's every word, eager to uncover the truth.

According to my mother, my aunt Norzie was a driven and ambitious woman with a clear vision for her future. From a young age, she had harbored dreams of owning her own public transport automobile, inspired by the entrepreneurial spirit that ran in our family.

Determined to turn her dreams into reality, my aunt worked tirelessly, accumulating a substantial sum of money through sheer hard work and determination. With her sights set on her goal, she was poised to embark on her entrepreneurial journey, ready to carve out a path of success and prosperity for herself.

However, fate had other plans. Love unexpectedly entered her life in the form of a devoted fiancé. As their relationship blossomed and deepened, my aunt found herself torn between her dreams of financial independence and her desire to build a life with her beloved.

In a moment of decision, my grandmother and aunt made a fateful choice, entrusting their hard-earned money to my aunt's fiancé with the intention of using it to purchase the commercial automobile that would launch her entrepreneurial career.

Tragically, their trust was betrayed. Consumed by greed and deceit, the fiancé absconded with the money, leaving my aunt and grandmother reeling from the betrayal. Overnight, their dreams lay shattered, and my aunt was left to pick up the pieces of her broken heart and fractured aspirations.

It was a story of love and loss, of dreams deferred and hopes dashed by the cruel hand of fate. And yet, despite the hardships she faced, my aunt Norzie remained steadfast in her resolve, refusing to let the betrayal of the past define her future. She continued to work hard, though her efforts seemed only to amount to nothing.

The Action of the Fiancé Disrupted My Aunt's Life

As I listened to my mother's words, I gained a newfound appreciation for the strength and resilience that defined my aunt's character. Though her path had been fraught with challenges and setbacks, she had never lost sight of her dreams. Her unwavering determination served as an inspiration to us all.

As my aunt Norzie bid farewell to her beloved fiancé, her heart swelled with anticipation and excitement for the bright future that lay ahead. With dreams of a new chapter in her life dancing before her eyes, she watched as he departed for the city, carrying with him the weight of their shared aspirations and hopes for the future.

In her mind's eye, she envisioned the bustling streets of the city, teeming with opportunity and promise, where they would soon embark on their journey to purchase the public transport automobile of their dreams. With each passing moment, her excitement grew, buoyed by the belief that their love would conquer all obstacles and pave the way for a prosperous and happy life together.

As the days turned into weeks, my aunt eagerly awaited news from her fiancé, clinging to the promise of his return and the fulfillment of their shared dreams. However, as the weeks stretched into months without a word from him, a gnawing sense of unease began to settle over her heart.

With each passing day, her hopes waned, replaced by a growing sense of apprehension and doubt. What had become of her beloved fiancé, and why had he not returned as promised? Questions swirled in her mind, casting a shadow of uncertainty over her once-bright and hopeful future.

Then, one fateful day, the truth was revealed in a cruel twist of fate. Word reached my aunt that her fiancé had absconded with the sack of money, leaving her and my grandmother betrayed and devastated by his deceit.

In an instant, her dreams lay shattered, her heart broken by the betrayal of the one she had loved and trusted above all else. As she grappled with the harsh reality of her situation, my aunt found herself thrust into a world of pain and uncertainty, forced to confront the unforgiving realities of love and loss.

Yet amidst the wreckage of her shattered dreams, my aunt Norzie found the strength to pick herself up and forge ahead, her spirit unbroken by the trials of the past. Though the road ahead was fraught with challenges and obstacles, she refused to let the betrayal define her future, determined to carve out a path of resilience and redemption in the face of adversity.

As the months turned into years, her anticipation gradually morphed into despair. With each passing day that her beloved failed to return, the weight of his absence bore down upon her spirit like a heavy burden. The hope that had once buoyed her heart gave way to a deep-seated mistrust, casting a shadow of doubt over her ability to trust again.

The pain of abandonment seeped into the very core of her being, leaving scars that never fully healed. In the absence of closure or reconciliation, my aunt found herself trapped in a cycle of anguish and sorrow, unable to move past the betrayal that had shattered her heart.

As the years stretched on, she retreated further into herself, her once vibrant spirit dulled by the ache of loneliness and betrayal. The dreams of love and companionship that had once fueled her hopes for the future faded into distant memories, replaced by a sense of resignation to her solitary existence.

Despite her best efforts to find solace in caring for my grandmother, the emptiness that gnawed at her soul remained ever-present. The pain of inadequacy and unworthiness weighed heavily upon her, a constant reminder of the love she had lost and the dreams left unfulfilled.

And so, my aunt spent her days in quiet resignation, her heart hardened by the scars of the past. Though she lived a life of devotion and selflessness, her pain remained unspoken, hidden beneath a veneer of stoicism and strength.

As the years turned into decades, my aunt's world grew smaller, her hopes for a brighter future dimming with each passing year. When she passed away at the age of 80, she left behind a legacy of resilience and perseverance—a testament to the enduring power of the human spirit in the face of adversity.

Though her life was marked by pain and loss, my aunt Norzie's story serves as a poignant reminder of the fragility of love and the profound impact of betrayal. While she may never have found the love she so desperately sought, her spirit lives on in the hearts of those who loved her—a beacon of hope and strength in the face of life's greatest challenges.

Attention

If you sense something amiss concerning a family member, do not hesitate to delve into your family history. Even if it's a taboo topic or one that others are reluctant to discuss, proceed with caution but remain persistent. Trust your instincts and seek the truth, no matter how uncomfortable it may be.

Understanding your family's history can provide valuable insights and potentially uncover hidden truths that may be influencing your present circumstances.

CHAPTER IV

My Sisters' Life's Story

Despite witnessing the success of my parents' marriage, it seemed that the same grace was not bestowed upon the daughters' relationships. Growing up, I had the privilege of witnessing the beautiful love story between my parents unfold before my eyes. My father embodied the role of the patriarch, deeply devoted to my mother with unwavering passion. In turn, my mother embraced her role as a submissive yet powerful wife, fulfilling her duties as a true helpmate, as God intended.

Their love was palpable, a force that permeated every corner of our home. Even in my mother's absence for just a day, her presence was sorely missed, leaving a noticeable void in our family dynamic. Despite marrying young—my father at 24 and my mother at 18—their bond endured for over 50 years until God called them home.

Their marriage was a testament to the enduring power of love, commitment, and faithfulness. Though I longed to emulate their example in my own life, fate seemed to have different plans for me, and I struggled to find the same level of harmony and fulfillment in my own relationships.

Attention

I have come to realize the importance of impartation. The Bible discusses many powerful servants of God, such as Abraham, Isaac, and Jacob, who, before their departure, assembled their children to impart blessings and wisdom. Unfortunately, my parents were unaware of these principles.

Beloved, there are blessings in your family that need to be intentionally imparted. While curses can perpetuate through the enemy's influence until someone breaks them, blessings require deliberate effort to maintain. Anything great requires diligence and effort to uphold.

Parents, if God has blessed you with a good marriage, ensure that you intentionally teach and impart this blessing to your biological and spiritual children, as the Bible instructs: "You shall teach them diligently to your children, and shall talk of them when you sit in your house, when you walk by the way, when you lie down, and when you rise up" (Deuteronomy 6:7).

First Sister

My eldest sister's journey into marriage diverged significantly from the path my parents had envisioned for her. At the age of 18, she decided to marry, despite my parents' strong objections to her choice of partner. Determined to follow her own heart, she proceeded with the marriage ceremony in the absence of our parents, who were deeply disheartened by her defiance.

As the first child and daughter in our family, her decision weighed heavily on my parents, leaving them profoundly disappointed in her choice of husband. Despite their reservations, my sister remained committed to her marriage, embarking on the daunting yet rewarding journey of motherhood and ultimately raising ten children.

However, despite the outward appearance of stability and the blessings of a large family, my sister's life lacked the elusive "happily ever after." Despite her best efforts and sacrifices, she grappled with challenges and hardships, never quite finding the fulfillment and contentment she had hoped for.

Tragically, her story came to an end recently with her passing, leaving behind a legacy tinged with both the joys and sorrows of a life lived with determination and resilience in the face of challenges. Her memory serves as a poignant reminder of the complexities of love, family, and the pursuit of happiness amidst life's unpredictable twists and turns.

Second Sister

The marriage of my fifth sibling, the second daughter, remains vivid in my memory, despite my tender age at the time. I had the honor of serving as the ring bearer, witnessing a ceremony filled with love and promise.

This sister possessed my parents' entrepreneurial spirit from a young age, reflecting the strength and determination of our mother. She carved her own path, achieving financial success through hard work and dedication. Yet, even with her accomplishments, she was not immune to the challenges that seemed to plague our family.

Despite her resilience and achievements, the cycle of hardship and disappointment persisted, casting a shadow over her life. Though she made every effort to break free from the constraints of our family's history, she found herself ensnared by the same trials and tribulations that had affected those before her.

Immediately following her marriage, my sister was confronted with a harsh reality: she barely knew the man she had wed. What began as a union filled with hope and promise quickly unraveled as she uncovered a web of deceit and hidden lies, eroding the trust and bond between her and her husband.

Ultimately, the marriage ended in divorce after my sister made the decision to leave Haiti and start anew in the United States. Determined to reclaim her entrepreneurial spirit and financial independence, she embarked on a journey marked by resilience and determination. However, her path was fraught with challenges. She encountered men who only served to dim her light, perpetuating the cycle of disappointment and disillusionment. Despite her efforts to escape the constraints of her past, she found herself trapped in a familiar pattern of unfulfilled promises and shattered dreams.

My sister's second marriage seemed to offer a glimmer of hope as she tied the knot with a man who purported to be devoutly religious. Yet, beneath the facade of piety lurked a wolf disguised in sheep's clothing. This man, if not for the divine intervention of God's grace, would have brought nothing but total destruction upon my sister's life.

For her, the trials and tribulations of womanhood were especially brutal. Despite her resilience and unwavering spirit, the challenges she faced were relentless and unforgiving. My sister was a fighter in every sense of the word; she stumbled but always found the strength to rise again. Yet, the limitations and setbacks she encountered seemed inescapable, weaving themselves into the very fabric of her existence.

I vividly remember the early days of my marriage. Just two months in, this sister called me with the intention of speaking a spell over my marriage. Over the phone, she said, "Your marriage will not work; do not be happy yet. Things will turn upside down for you soon." It was a stark moment—a reminder of the truth that people can only exude the state of their own souls.

She often spoke of how our older sister used to speak ill of her, perpetuating a cycle of negativity. This reinforced the saying, *"Hurt people hurt people."* Her life was marred by turmoil and chaos, making it difficult for her to digest my success and happiness in relationships.

Her actions, driven by her own pain, underscored a profound truth: people can only pass on who they are. This perpetuates family patterns, both positive and negative, across generations. The pain and dysfunction that plagued my sister's life had been handed down, creating a cycle that seemed unbreakable. These patterns lock family dynamics in a seemingly endless loop, perpetuating the same struggles and hardships.

Insights

It is not until someone receives the grace from the Lord to confront these patterns head-on that real change can occur. Tackling these deep-rooted issues from their very foundation is no small feat. It requires immense courage, resilience, and a willingness to face the discomfort of confronting long-standing family issues.

Embarking on this journey of breaking generational cycles is anything but easy. It involves digging deep into the roots of familial pain, understanding its origins, and actively working to transform those patterns. It is a path filled with emotional labor, self-reflection, and often, a great deal of heartache. However, it is also a path of profound healing and liberation.

By addressing these ingrained patterns, we begin to rewrite the narrative for ourselves and future generations. This journey is about more than just personal healing; it is about creating a new legacy—one where peace, love, and understanding replace chaos and pain.

Reflecting on my own experience, I recognize the power of grace in this transformative process. It is the grace that allows me to see beyond the hurt, to understand the reasons behind the actions of others, and to find the strength to change the course of my own life. Through this grace, one can break free from the chains of the past and pave the way for a brighter, more harmonious future.

Third Sister

The marriage of my eighth sibling, the third daughter, remains etched in my memory. I recall her radiant beauty—tall, slender, with cascading ebony hair reminiscent of Indian silk. She was a woman of God, driven by ambition, relentlessly pursuing her dreams as a kindergarten teacher until she encountered a man who dragged her down into the depths of despair.

Despite the challenges she faced, including the birth of six beautiful daughters, she remained committed to her marriage. I watched firsthand as she navigated the treacherous waters of a difficult relationship, striving to make it work against all odds.

However, the curse that seemed to afflict our family persisted, as she found herself entangled with a man who mirrored the same destructive patterns that women in our family seem to attract — "men that are destiny destroyers." Men who fall short of fulfilling their mission. Despite her efforts, the cycle continued, leaving her longing for a happiness that always seemed just out of reach.

Though she remains married to this day, my sister has yet to find the elusive "happily ever after" she so desperately deserves. However, amidst life's trials and tribulations, she remains a beacon of faith—a true woman of

God. I have witnessed her unwavering resilience, drawing strength from her deep-rooted connection with the divine. Yet, despite her steadfastness, the insidious grip of familial patterns continues to linger.

The pattern, it seems, did not escape her. Unbeknownst to her, she inadvertently perpetuates the very cycles she endured. It is a revelation that eludes her, shrouded in the veil of unawareness. Looking back, it seems as if everyone in our family walked with their heads in a sack, oblivious to the intricate web of generational dynamics at play. We were all blind to the cyclical nature of our behaviors, trapped in a perpetual loop of dysfunction.

Insights

In the midst of this collective blindness, self-blame becomes a familiar companion, and guilt, shame, and bitterness take root in the depths of our souls. We embark on a journey of internal turmoil, each step laden with the weight of unresolved emotions. Yet, despite our fervent search for answers, the root cause remains elusive, obscured by layers of familial history and intergenerational trauma.

Breaking free from this cycle requires a courageous act of self-discovery and introspection. It demands that we confront the shadows of our past, shining a light on the hidden corners of our psyche. It is a journey fraught with uncertainty—a pilgrimage into the depths of our being, where truth and revelation await.

With each step forward, we inch closer to liberation, unraveling the tangled threads of familial patterns that bind us. It is a process of reclaiming our power, forging a new path unencumbered by the ghosts of the past. Moreover, in this journey of self-discovery, we find solace in the embrace of divine grace—a guiding light illuminating the way forward.

As we navigate the labyrinth of our own souls, we emerge transformed—reborn from the ashes of our past. We stand tall, no longer shackled by the chains of generational patterns, but empowered by the wisdom gained through our journey. In this newfound freedom, we pave the way for future generations to break free from the cycles of old, forging a legacy of healing, resilience, and redemption.

In the end, it is through our collective journey of self-discovery and healing that we transcend the limitations of our past, embracing the infinite possibilities of the future. Though the road ahead may be fraught with challenges, we walk it with courage and conviction, knowing that with each step, we draw closer to the destined life that God has ordained for us.

Attention

Recognizing the repetitive patterns in the women in my family's relationships was a revelation in itself. It became evident that their experiences were not mere coincidences or strokes of bad luck. Instead, there seemed to be a darker force at play, orchestrating their romantic encounters and marital struggles. While my sisters may have overlooked these patterns, I could not ignore them. However, understanding the pattern was only the first step; breaking free from its grip would prove to be a far more daunting challenge.

CHAPTER V

Story of Some of Rich Women in My Family

Delving deeper into the history of the women in my father's family revealed a striking pattern. There were two prominent women who achieved remarkable success in both business and marriage. They amassed wealth, owned numerous properties, and led seemingly fulfilling lives. However, their success was tragically short-lived, as they passed away prematurely. Reflecting on their lives, I couldn't help but question why these accomplished women met such untimely ends.

The realization struck me: why did these successful women face such unfortunate fates? Moreover, why did this curse seem to disproportionately afflict the women in my family, likely sparing the men who enjoyed success in both marriage and finance without facing similar repercussions? These questions lingered in my mind, urging me to uncover the underlying forces at play and motivating me to break free from this cycle of misfortune.

In contrast to the trend observed in my father's family, a similar pattern emerged in my mother's lineage regarding unfulfilled relationships. However, what set them apart was their resilience and strong personalities. Despite encountering challenges in their marriages, they displayed remarkable strength and determination, often leading to more successful unions.

Unlike the women in my father's family, who appeared to yield to external pressures, the women in my mother's family stood steadfast against adversity. Their robust personalities enabled them to navigate through turbulent times in their relationships, fostering greater stability and resilience in their marriages. This disparity underscores the significance of inner strength and resilience in overcoming familial patterns and breaking free from cycles of misfortune.

Attention

Embracing the truth of one's familial history is a powerful step toward personal growth and transformation. It's essential not to let the past define you, but instead, use it as a stepping stone to move forward with strength and determination.

Instructing oneself in the teachings of great men and women of God can be a source of inspiration and guidance on this journey. For me, embracing the instructions of men like Prophet Lovy Elias, Pastor Gregory Toussaint, Prophet Jules Dessin, and TB Joshua, as well as immersing myself in the teachings of experienced women of God such as Prophetess Maggy Ellias, the matriarch of Revelation Church, and Joyce Meyer, Prophetess Kathrin Kaulman, Rose Kelvin, and others, has been instrumental.

These spiritual leaders may not be physically close to us, but through their teachings and the grace of God upon their lives, we can receive impartation and wisdom. Whether it's listening to sermons, reading their books, or attending their services, there are various ways to connect with their teachings and apply them to our own lives.

By embracing and appreciating the grace of God upon their lives, we open ourselves up to receive the same grace and wisdom. It's a journey of spiritual growth and transformation, where each step brings us closer to breaking free from familial patterns and living a life of purpose and fulfillment.

Be Imparted by Honoring Women of God

Honoring women of God in our lives can indeed be a source of profound wisdom and guidance. For me, my mother stands out as a remarkable role model. From a young age, I witnessed her unwavering commitment to her marriage and family.

Married at the tender age of 18, my mother embarked on a journey of love and partnership with my father, a man of God who cherished her deeply. Their marriage spanned over 50 years, marked by mutual respect, love, and devotion. While they were not without flaws, their commitment to each other was unwavering.

My mother's example taught me invaluable lessons about what it means to cultivate a healthy and fulfilling relationship. She was the pillar of our family, demonstrating the importance of communication, compromise, and unconditional love. Through her actions, she showed me that a successful marriage isn't about perfection but about the mutual willingness to support, uplift, and grow together.

In honoring and emulating the women of God in our lives, we gain insight into the dynamics of healthy relationships and learn how to navigate the challenges that come our way. My mother's legacy continues to inspire me, serving as a guiding light as I strive to build strong and lasting connections in my own life.

Absolutely, finding inspiration and guidance from various sources can be incredibly enriching. Whether it is a pastor's wife, a family member, or prominent figures like Michelle Obama, Mirlande Manigat, Hillary Clinton, or Barbara Bush, there's much to learn from their experiences and wisdom.

Studying their behaviors, reading their books, and observing how they navigate their relationships can offer valuable insights into what it takes to cultivate successful and fulfilling partnerships. By discerning the qualities, attitudes, and actions that contribute to their success, we can glean lessons that align with our own values and aspirations.

Ultimately, drawing from the experiences of these women allows us to expand our perspectives, deepen our understanding of relationships, and gain wisdom that can positively influence our own journey toward building meaningful and lasting connections.

CHAPTER VI

My Own Story of Marriage

Arriving in the USA as a young girl, my primary goal was to serve God with all my heart. However, attending church posed a challenge due to transportation constraints, as I desired to be present not only on Sundays but also during the weekdays. Despite this obstacle, a turning point came when I was introduced to a pastor who, in turn, connected me with a church bus driver. This connection proved invaluable, enabling me to attend church regularly, even for weekday services, fulfilling my earnest desire to be actively engaged in worship and fellowship.

I was exhilarated by this newfound freedom to attend church regularly, immersing myself in each service and finding immense joy in being present. It was during one of these church visits that I first encountered the gentleman who would later become my husband. At that time, we were both very young, full of excitement about what the future held. Our initial meeting marked the beginning of a journey that would see us dating for several years, each moment filled with anticipation and hope for what lay ahead.

Being a part of this church was an integral aspect of my life. I threw myself into various roles and activities, immersing myself in the vibrant community. I was an active member of the choir and participated in singing groups like the praise team, as well as other forming groups. Beyond music, I also engaged in leading services, attending youth meetings, and participating in church cleanings and other activities.

The church became my sanctuary, my refuge from the chaos of the world. I cherished every moment spent within its walls, finding solace and fulfillment in serving the Lord and being surrounded by fellow believers. It was a place where my spirit felt alive, where I could express my love for God freely and without reservation. I dedicated much of my time to the church, yet I never felt weary or drained; instead, each moment only fueled my passion and devotion further.

Our journey together took a significant turn when this young man pursued me, and we began dating. However, even the dating period came with its challenges. One notable incident occurred when the church leaders decided that we should get married. Despite having been in a relationship for a couple of years, we felt unprepared for marriage. We were still young, with limited financial resources, and hadn't yet completed college. Despite these reservations, an ultimatum was issued, urging us to marry, even though there was no immediate urgency for such a decision.

Our marriage began on what felt like the wrong foot, with a sense of being pressured and sabotaged by external forces. At the time, I failed to realize that it was the work of the enemy at play. However, I'm not here to place blame. Despite the difficulties and eventual dissolution of the marriage, I've come to understand that forgiveness is key.

Just like the other women in my family, even though I was very young at 20 years old and had just migrated to America, by the grace of God, I started working right away and saved a significant amount of money relatively quickly. When I was about to get married four years later, my immigration process was not yet complete. Therefore, I entrusted all my savings to my soon-to-be husband to buy a house in his name only. My bank account, my paid-off car, and the house were all under his name.

Avoiding the finer details, shortly after our marriage, my savings dissipated within a few months. He convinced me to sell the car, and after our divorce, he claimed ownership of the house and still lives in it to this day. Plus, guess what? He told me, "Did you have a house under your name?" The fact that I trusted him before marriage to buy it without including me meant I had no claim to it.

It is the same scenario that has been happening to the women in my family over and over again. This cycle of misplaced trust and financial vulnerability has plagued us for generations. Despite my efforts to break free from this pattern, I found myself entangled in a similar situation. The lessons of my past and the stories of the women before me serve as a painful reminder of the importance of safeguarding one's assets and ensuring that trust is not misplaced.

Reflecting on my past, I have realized that I had the willingness but lacked the power to escape the situation, even amidst the challenges. While my marriage was marred by hardship, I choose to forgive my ex-husband completely.

Through this journey, I have learned invaluable lessons that have shaped me into the person I am today. Also, it is all part of the journey.

The Journey After the Divorce

Following my divorce, I found myself grappling with the painful realization that the pattern of my family history had repeated itself in my own life. This recognition left me feeling bitter and questioning why God would allow such hardship to befall me, especially considering my unwavering love and service to Him.

Despite being aware of the choices of men that had plagued my family's history, I still found myself entangled with a similar individual. This realization stirred a sense of frustration and disappointment within me, as I grappled with the implications of repeating the same cycle that had afflicted generations before me.

Amidst my struggles, I faced harsh judgments and condemnation from fellow Christians within the church community. It was disheartening to witness how some members of our faith were quick to cast stones and pass judgment without seeking to understand the truth or the underlying reasons behind my circumstances.

Instead of offering support and compassion during my time of need, I was met with condemnation from those who should have extended love and understanding. It was a stark reminder of how some individuals within the Christian community prioritize judgment over compassion, failing to embody the true essence of Christ's teachings.

Despite the judgment and condemnation, I faced from fellow believers, I continued to attend church because I knew I had nowhere else to turn. Yet, the weight of their disapproval lingered within me. Deep down, I grappled with a haunting question: would I ever regain the ability to preach the gospel, lead services, sing in the choir, or serve in God's kingdom again?

Each day felt like traversing through a dense fog of uncertainty and doubt, with a dark cloud of shame trailing behind me wherever I went. The once-vibrant spirit that propelled me to actively engage in church activities now felt suffocated by the weight of judgment and condemnation.

The Strength of the Chosen Ones

God never leaves nor forsakes the chosen ones. After the divorce, though I felt defeated in my spiritual life, I refused to give up. Determined to rebuild, I worked two jobs. Within three months, God blessed me with a better and bigger house to live in. I barely suffered from financial hardship during this time; God took care of me. I'm grateful!

He guided my path as a registered nurse, providing opportunities and stability in my career. Despite the challenges, He ensured that my son and I were well taken care of. His grace and provision were evident in every aspect of our lives. Through His unwavering support, I found the strength to persevere and thrive, reminding me of His constant presence and faithfulness.

Revelation

Honoring and revering others in successful relationships is one of the keys to receiving impartation and grace, both materially and spiritually. Whether it is a parent, child, family member, brethren, or even a stranger, the principle remains the same: when we hold others in high regard, it opens the door for blessings to flow into our lives.

Even in the context of marriage, where discord may exist without violence, fostering a culture of honor and reverence can transform the dynamics of the relationship. By showing genuine respect and admiration for our spouses and other exemplars in our lives, we create an environment conducive to receiving blessings and grace.

The key is authenticity; our reverence must be sincere and heartfelt. When we genuinely honor and revere others, we create a positive energy that attracts blessings and favor into our lives. It is a universal principle that transcends boundaries and applies to all aspects of our relationships.

So, let us cultivate a spirit of honor and reverence in our interactions with others, recognizing the inherent value and dignity in each person we encounter. In doing so, we open ourselves up to a world of blessings and grace beyond measure.

CHAPTER VII

Honor for My Parents

It's a profound observation to recognize the lack of honor in family relationships, especially when it comes to acknowledging the harmony, efforts, and strengths of our parents' relationship. In many families, the importance of honoring relationships is often overlooked or undervalued, leading to a disconnect in understanding the significance of impartation and grace.

In the case of my parents, who were able to cultivate a strong and enduring bond, their example should have been revered and celebrated by the rest of the family. Their commitment, love, and resilience in their marriage should have served as a beacon of inspiration for their children, imparting invaluable wisdom and grace for building successful relationships.

However, if this honor was not bestowed upon them, it's likely that their ability to impart their wisdom and grace to their children was hindered. Without the acknowledgment and respect, they deserved, their influence may have been limited, and the opportunity to learn from their experiences may have been lost.

Recognizing this deficiency in honoring relationships within the family is the first step toward rectifying it. By acknowledging the strength and value of our parents' relationship, we can begin to honor their legacy and learn from their example. This acknowledgment opens the door for impartation, allowing us to receive the grace and wisdom needed to build strong, healthy relationships of our own.

Moving forward, it is essential to instill a culture of honor and reverence within the family, not only towards our parents but towards each other as well. By honoring the relationships that have shaped us and recognizing the value they bring to our lives, we create an environment where impartation can flourish, leading to greater understanding, connection, and fulfillment within the family unit.

My first sister got married without their approval, meaning they did not release any blessing on their union. Though I was not yet born when she got married, I've heard the story. At my second sister's wedding, where I was the ring bearer, I can clearly recall that there was no counsel or blessing given. My third sister's wedding was hastily arranged, and my father couldn't even attend. While my mother offered support, she didn't serve as an imparter. Due to the distance of another country, my parents couldn't attend my wedding. Despite this, impartation could have occurred, but at the time, I neither knew nor cared about it.

For years, my family failed to recognize the recurring pattern in our relationships until God unveiled it to me. It became clear that while my mother had been blessed with a remarkable husband—a handsome, tall, God-fearing man who was a great provider and loved her deeply for over half a century—none of us had experienced such grace in our own unions. Reflecting on this revelation, it became evident that we had overlooked the significance of their bond and failed to appreciate the blessings that stemmed from their enduring marriage.

Indeed, the concept of impartation is deeply rooted in biblical tradition. Throughout the Scriptures, we encounter numerous instances where blessings and prayers are imparted from one generation to the next. For example, Abraham, the patriarch of the Israelites, played a pivotal role in ensuring the continuation of his lineage by sending his servants to find a suitable wife for his son, Isaac. Similarly, Isaac imparted blessings to his sons, Jacob and Esau, before his death, shaping the trajectory of their lives and the future of their descendants. This pattern of impartation is further exemplified in the lives of other biblical figures, underscoring its significance in passing down blessings, guidance, and spiritual authority from one generation to another.

Absolutely, honoring the grace on others is key to receiving similar blessings in our own lives. It's never too late to start cultivating this practice. Whether it's someone close to you or a respected figure from afar, honoring them can pave the way for divine impartation.

Expressing honor can take various forms, from offering gifts and acts of kindness to seeking their prayers and blessings. Even if they are unaware of you, genuine honor has a transformative power that transcends physical proximity. Over time, as you continue to honor them sincerely, you will begin to partake in their grace and blessings.

This principle of honoring those who carry the grace of healthy relationships is a timeless truth that holds the potential to usher in positive changes and blessings in our own lives.

Attention

Don't allow anyone or anything to hinder you from answering the call of God on your life. I learned this lesson the hard way, wasting precious time that could have been spent serving in God's kingdom. The enemy's plan is to distract you with darkness and obstacles, preventing you from fulfilling your destiny. However, don't succumb to these distractions. Stay focused.

Remember, there is no stain of the enemy that the blood of Jesus cannot wash away. Jesus bore all shame and humiliation on the cross for us, and if we follow Him faithfully, we will overcome every obstacle. Your destiny is bright, and the call of God on your life is unmistakable. Do not give up or surrender to the challenges you face. Shake off the negativity and press forward.

As you say yes to the Lord and follow His lead, the rewards will not only be evident in your life but will also impact generations to come. So, pick yourself up, keep moving forward, and trust that God has a plan and purpose for your life that far exceeds any obstacle or setback you may encounter.

Courage Needed to Break Vicious Cycles

Breaking familial cycles of misfortune necessitates a comprehensive approach that incorporates various elements. While the divine hand plays a pivotal role and serves as the foundational force, it alone may not suffice to eliminate entrenched patterns. Alongside divine intervention, it requires a concerted effort characterized by discipline, motivation, determination, guidance, and a clear vision.

Discipline is essential in maintaining consistency and adhering to the steps necessary for breaking free from familial cycles. It involves committing to new habits, routines, and mindsets that align with the desired outcome of breaking the cycle.

Motivation serves as the driving force behind one's efforts to break free from these patterns. It stems from a deep-rooted desire for change and a willingness to put in the necessary work and effort despite obstacles and setbacks.

Determination is the unwavering resolve to persevere in the face of challenges and adversity. It entails staying focused on the goal of breaking free from familial patterns and refusing to be deterred by setbacks or obstacles along the way.

Guidance and instruction provide valuable insight and support in navigating the complexities of familial dynamics and ingrained patterns. Seeking counsel from trusted mentors, spiritual leaders, or therapists can offer fresh perspectives and strategies for breaking free from these cycles.

A clear vision serves as a guiding beacon, illuminating the path forward and providing a sense of purpose and direction. It involves envisioning a future free from the constraints of familial patterns and embracing the possibility of positive change and transformation.

By combining these elements—divine intervention, discipline, motivation, determination, guidance, and a clear vision—one can effectively uproot the unfortunate cycles of misfortune that have plagued their family lineage. It is through this holistic approach that lasting change and freedom from familial patterns can be achieved.

Ready-Set-Go

Upon discovering the recurring patterns within the women of my family, I was filled with a resolute determination to break the cycle once and for all. With every fiber of my being, I declared that this legacy of misfortune would not be passed down to my son or future generations.

I refused to accept that these patterns were inevitable or beyond my control. Instead, I embraced the belief that men like my father, possessing admirable qualities such as a great personality, devotion to God, industriousness, responsibility, and being a provider and protector, were not merely outliers, but a testament to the potential for positive change within our lineage.

With this conviction firmly entrenched in my heart and mind, I embarked on a journey of self-discovery, introspection, and transformation. I committed myself to embodying the qualities of resilience, strength, and perseverance that had characterized the women in my mother's family.

Furthermore, I sought to cultivate a clear vision of a future untethered by the constraints of familial patterns, envisioning a legacy of love, stability, and success for my son and generations to come. This vision served as a guiding light, illuminating the path forward and motivating me to take the necessary steps to break free from the cycles of misfortune that had plagued my family for generations.

Through unwavering determination, steadfast faith, and a commitment to positive change, I forged ahead, determined to rewrite the narrative of my family's history and create a legacy defined by hope, resilience, and triumph.

In a decisive moment of clarity and determination, I made a solemn vow to myself: I would not settle for anything less than the best. With unwavering resolve, I declared that the cycle of unfortunate relationships with men of shallow character and empty promises would end with me.

I refused to succumb to the patterns of the past, recognizing that true fulfillment and happiness could only be found by breaking free from the shackles of generational misfortune. Armed with this newfound determination, I began to speak my intentions into existence, affirming with every word that the cycle of toxic relationships would cease to exist from that moment forward.

Despite the allure of superficial traits such as education and physical attractiveness displayed by these men, I understood that true worth lay far beyond the surface. I refused to be swayed by external appearances or empty promises, recognizing that lasting fulfillment could only be found in relationships built on God's presence, mutual respect, integrity, and genuine love.

With each declaration, I set in motion a powerful transformation, laying the foundation for a new beginning characterized by love, respect, and fulfillment. I refused to allow the shortcomings of the past to dictate the course of my future, embracing the power of my words to shape my reality and create a life filled with love, joy, and purpose.

In my quest to break free from the cycles of misfortune that had plagued my family for generations, I embarked on a journey of fasting and prayer. With each passing day of fasting, I felt myself drawing closer to the divine purpose that had long eluded me.

In addition to fasting, I made a conscious effort to keep myself pure, both in body and spirit. I focused intently on the calling that God had placed upon my life—a calling I had neglected for far too long. As I immersed myself in God's word and sought His guidance through prayer, I felt a renewed sense of purpose and clarity begin to emerge within me.

Alongside my spiritual disciplines, I actively sought out relationships with individuals who shared my faith and values. I surrounded myself with men and women of integrity and character, forging deep and meaningful connections that uplifted and inspired me.

As I cultivated these relationships, I began to notice a shift in the patterns of love that had plagued my family for generations. The toxic and destructive relationships that had once held sway over my life began to fade into the background, replaced by a newfound sense of peace and contentment.

Moreover, I had the privilege of crossing paths with servants of God who embraced me with genuine friendship and support. These spiritual mentors and guides became pillars of strength and wisdom, guiding me along the path toward healing and wholeness.

Through fasting, prayer, and the cultivation of meaningful relationships, I found myself gradually breaking free from the chains of generational misfortune. With each step forward, I drew closer to the divine destiny that awaited me, empowered by the love and grace of a God who had never abandoned me.

In the midst of my spiritual journey, a profound transformation began to take place within me. With each passing day, I found myself experiencing a newfound sense of trust and clarity that had long eluded me.

One of the most significant changes I noticed was my ability to trust again. After suffering from betrayal and disappointment, I had built walls around my heart, wary of allowing anyone to get too close. However, as I delved deeper into my relationship with God, I discovered a renewed capacity for trust—both in Him and in the people He brought into my life.

Moreover, I began to develop a heightened sense of discernment, enabling me to see people for who they truly are, without judgment or prejudice. Instead of trying to change others to fit my expectations, I learned to accept them as they are, flaws and all. This newfound acceptance allows me to love others from a distance, without feeling the need to control or change them.

As I embraced this mindset of acceptance and authenticity, I found myself no longer wasting time with people who did not appreciate or respect me. I realized that everyone has the right to their own opinions and preferences, and I chose to surround myself only with those who valued and respected me for who I was.

In cultivating my inner circle, I prioritized relationships based on mutual respect and admiration. I surrounded myself with individuals who uplifted and inspired me, and who shared my values and aspirations. In turn, I offered them the same level of respect and appreciation, creating a supportive network of like-minded individuals who encouraged and empowered one another.

Through this process of self-discovery and transformation, I learned the importance of setting boundaries and prioritizing my own well-being. By embracing authenticity, acceptance, and discernment, I found myself breaking free from the patterns of dysfunction that had plagued my family for generations, paving the way for a future filled with love, fulfillment, and purpose.

As I immersed myself deeper into my mission in Christ, my priorities shifted, and my time became increasingly precious. I found myself fully engaged in the work of God, dedicating my days to serving others and spreading His message of love and salvation. In the midst of this newfound purpose, I began to experience a profound sense of contentment and fulfillment that I had never known before.

With each passing day, my small circles of friends grew tighter, and my relationships became more meaningful. I found myself surrounded by individuals who shared my values and supported me in my journey, uplifting me with their encouragement and companionship.

As I continued to walk in faith, my confidence began to blossom, rooted in the unwavering knowledge that I was exactly where God wanted me to be. I no longer felt the need to seek validation or approval from others, as my sense of self-worth was firmly grounded in my identity as a child of God.

However, this transformation did not happen overnight. It was the result of a period of soul-searching, prayer, and self-reflection, coupled with the boundless grace and love of God. Each step of the way, I faced challenges and obstacles that tested my resolve, but I persevered, knowing that God was guiding me every step of the way.

Through His grace, I found the strength to overcome my fears and insecurities, embracing my true identity and stepping into the fullness of His purpose for my life. As I continued to walk in obedience to His will, I experienced a joy and peace that surpassed all understanding, knowing that I was exactly where I was meant to be.

CHAPTER VIII

Attention for Women

If you find yourself as a woman in the position of recognizing destructive patterns or curses within your family, remember that you also possess the power to break those cycles. Just as you have identified the snake, you also have the ability to overcome it.

This realization is not merely about recognizing the negative patterns; it is about taking decisive action to eradicate them. It requires courage, determination, and a deep-seated belief in God and in your own ability to effect change.

By acknowledging the presence of these destructive patterns, you have already taken the first step toward liberation. Now, armed with this awareness, you can begin the process of dismantling these cycles, one step at a time.

Whether it's through prayer, fasting, seeking counsel, or taking practical steps to change your circumstances, know that you have the power to break free from the grip of generational curses.

Embrace your role as a catalyst for change in your family's narrative. With God's guidance and your unwavering determination, you can overcome any obstacle and pave the way for a brighter, more fulfilling future for yourself and future generations.

As women, we are designed to be helpers as well as leaders in our own right. However, if you find yourself repeatedly encountering men who exhibit selfishness, emotional unavailability, and a lack of responsibility or protection, it's essential to recognize this pattern.

Remember that men do not necessarily need to be your romantic partners to demonstrate a sense of responsibility towards you. Whether they are family, friends, colleagues, or acquaintances, their behavior towards you should reflect mutual respect and care.

If you find yourself stuck in a cycle of attracting the wrong type of men, it may be necessary to take a step back and evaluate your own boundaries, self-worth, and the qualities you value in relationships.

Do not be afraid to set high standards for yourself and those you allow into your life. Surround yourself with people who uplift and empower you, and do not settle for anything less than you deserve. With self-awareness, self-love, and a firm belief in your worth, you can break free from negative patterns and cultivate healthy, fulfilling relationships.

Indeed, it is natural and rewarding for men to protect and provide for women and children. However, if you consistently encounter men who behave wickedly or recklessly around you, whether they are family members, friends, or romantic partners, it is crucial to recognize that this is not normal or acceptable behavior.

While it seems true that there are both good and bad men in the world, if you find yourself repeatedly attracting negative individuals, it is worth examining what might be drawing them to you. Often, there are dark forces, underlying patterns, or dynamics at play that contribute to this cycle.

Self-reflection is key in understanding your own role in these interactions. Consider examining your boundaries, self-esteem, and the qualities you prioritize in relationships. Often, unconscious beliefs or past experiences may influence the types of people we attract into our lives.

By gaining clarity on what you truly value and deserve in relationships, you can begin to set healthier boundaries and make choices that align with your well-being and happiness. Surround yourself with individuals who uplift and respect you, and do not hesitate to distance yourself from those who do not. Remember, you have the power to cultivate positive and fulfilling relationships in your life.

Taking the time to investigate yourself and other family members can be a transformative journey. By delving into the history of the family, one can uncover patterns and dynamics that may have been overlooked or ignored. Understanding these familial patterns is the first step toward breaking free from them.

Insights

As the Bible says, "If you know the truth, the truth will make you free." This rings especially true when it comes to familial patterns and cycles. By gaining insight into the past, individuals can make informed decisions about their present and future.

However, this process requires courage, introspection, and a willingness to confront uncomfortable truths. It may involve uncovering painful memories or acknowledging difficult dynamics within the family. Yet, it is through this process of self-discovery and understanding that individuals can begin to break the cycle and chart a new path forward.

Ultimately, the goal is not to assign blame or dwell on past mistakes, but rather to learn from the past and create a brighter future. Armed with knowledge and awareness, individuals can make conscious choices to create healthier relationships and break free from the constraints of familial patterns.

Women as Helpmates

Ladies, let us take a moment to reflect on our God-given role as helpmates, a term used in the Bible to describe our purpose in supporting men. As it says in Genesis 2:18, *"Then the LORD God said, 'It is not good that the man should be alone; I will make him a helper fit for him.'"* This designation carries profound significance, deeply rooted in divine wisdom. Before we explore this role further, consider this: who else is described as a helper in Scripture? The answer is none other than God Himself.

In Hebrews 13:6, the scripture proclaims, *"The Lord is my helper; I will not fear; what can man do to me?"* Here, God declares Himself as our helper, offering protection, strength, and guidance. This portrayal of God as a helper reveals that the role of a helper is not one of weakness or inferiority, but of strength, support, and empowerment. As women, when we embrace this role, we align ourselves with God's own example of being a powerful force of assistance and encouragement.

Isaiah 41:10 further reinforces this idea, where God reassures us with His steadfast support: *"Fear not, for I am with you; be not dismayed, for I am your God; I will strengthen you, I will help you, I will uphold you with my righteous right hand."* These words are a divine reminder that God's help is always available, and it is through His strength that we find our own ability to help others.

Moreover, the concept of a helper is central to the New Testament as well. Jesus, in His divine wisdom, instructed His disciples to wait in Jerusalem until they received the Helper He promised—the Holy Spirit. In John 14:26, Jesus says, *"But the Helper, the Holy Spirit, whom the Father will send in My name, He will teach you all things, and bring to your remembrance all things that I said to you."* The Holy Spirit, as the ultimate helper, provides wisdom, guidance, and comfort, empowering the disciples to fulfill their mission.

In this light, we see that being a helper is not a secondary role but a vital one, filled with purpose and strength. The role of a helper is essential, not only in human relationships but also in the spiritual realm. Let us step confidently into this role, understanding that in doing so, we mirror the very nature of God Himself, who is our ultimate Helper and source of strength.

As women, understanding this divine dynamic between men and women can significantly reduce friction in our daily interactions—whether as spouses, coworkers, family members, friends, or acquaintances. It is important to note that this understanding does not imply that men are weak or incapable. On the contrary, it acknowledges that men carry a multitude of responsibilities and require support to manage them effectively.

When we embrace our role as helpers, we fulfill a crucial part of God's design, ensuring that both men and women can thrive in their unique capacities. This mutual dependence fosters a harmonious relationship where both genders can support and uplift each other, reflecting the divine balance God intended.

Attention for Men

Absolutely, the dynamics of relationships between men and women are often influenced by the sense of security, protection, and provision that men provide. If you consistently find yourself encountering disrespectful, demanding, and non-submissive women, it's essential to reflect on the energy you're putting out and the kind of relationships you're attracting.

As a man, it is important to recognize that women naturally gravitate towards men who offer a sense of security, stability, and leadership. When these elements are present, women are more inclined to be submissive and respectful in their interactions. However, if you find that women are bossing you around to fulfill their needs, it may indicate a misalignment in the dynamics of the relationship.

Taking a conscious approach to the energy you emit and the standards you uphold can significantly impact the type of women you attract. By embodying qualities of strength, integrity, and provision, you are more likely to draw in women who appreciate and value these attributes, fostering healthier and more fulfilling relationships.

The Bible provides guidance on the roles and responsibilities within a marital relationship. Men are instructed to love their wives sacrificially, just as Christ loved the church and gave Himself up for her. This kind of love is selfless, unconditional, and willing to make sacrifices for the well-being and happiness of the spouse (Genesis 2; Ephesians 5).

On the other hand, women are called to submit to their husbands. However, it's essential to understand that submission in this context does not imply inferiority or servitude. Instead, it's a mutual expression of love, respect, and partnership within the marriage. It's about willingly yielding to the leadership and authority of the husband, in a spirit of mutual submission and respect for God's ordained roles.

In a healthy marriage, both partners seek to honor and fulfill their roles as outlined in the Bible, understanding that their ultimate allegiance is to God. This mutual love, respect, and submission create a harmonious and fulfilling relationship that reflects the love and unity within the body of Christ.

Insights

Men as Leaders

Men are divinely called to be leaders, a role established from the very beginning in the book of Genesis. According to Scripture, Adam was created after God had formed everything else, entering a world that was already full of life and responsibility. This timing is significant; it signifies that men are naturally wired to lead, direct, provide, and protect. Leadership is an inherent quality in men, designed by God, and they are equipped to navigate their responsibilities without needing someone else to take the reins for them.

However, if you find yourself, as a man, in a position where you rely on a woman to provide for and protect you, it's worth considering whether you might be operating under spiritual or situational hindrances. While men certainly need women to assist and support them in their endeavors, women should not be the source of a man's provision and protection. In some circumstances, roles may vary due to life's complexities, but the fundamental principle remains: men are called to be leaders in their homes, workplaces, and communities.

Even in a professional setting where a woman may hold a leadership position, a man can still lead through his Christ-centered identity. By embodying the qualities of protection and provision within the appropriate context, a man can influence and lead with integrity, without undermining the authority of a female leader. Leadership, in this sense, is not about titles but about character and actions that align with God's design.

The principles of leadership are foundational to how society is structured. Men and women are created to complement one another, each playing unique and vital roles. However, there is a divine order to our interactions, regardless of the nature of our relationships—whether as spouses, colleagues, family members, friends, or acquaintances.

The Bible provides a clear outline of the qualities that men should embody as leaders. In 1 Timothy 3:1-7, it states: *"The saying is trustworthy: If anyone aspires to the office of overseer, he desires a noble task. Therefore, an overseer must be above reproach, the husband of one wife, sober-minded, self-controlled, respectable, hospitable, able to teach, not a drunkard, not violent but gentle, not quarrelsome, not a lover of money. He must manage his own household well, with all dignity keeping his children submissive, for if someone does not know how to manage his own household, how will he care for God's church?"*

This passage highlights the essential characteristics of a godly leader: integrity, self-control, respectability, and the ability to manage one's household. These traits are not just for those in formal positions of leadership within the church but are a model for all men. To lead effectively, men must first govern their own lives and homes with wisdom and grace. Only then can they extend that leadership to the broader community, fulfilling their God-given role with honor.

When I was growing up, I wasn't even aware of the biblical principles surrounding gender roles. Yet, I always found myself instinctively running to my father when I needed guidance or money, even though I had a nurturing mother. There was something about my father's presence that made me feel safe, both physically and spiritually. This sense of security came from knowing that my father was a godly man, and it shaped my experience of growing up as a young woman.

Finally, men are inherently equipped to lead and are called to do so with strength, wisdom, and a deep sense of responsibility. While women play an indispensable role in supporting and complementing men, the divine order places men in a position to lead. By embracing this role, men can fulfill their purpose and contribute to a harmonious and well-ordered society, as intended by God.

Men and Women as a Team

In today's world, many modern women claim that they can do what men can do, and sometimes even do it better. In some instances, this is true; as helpmates, women often grasp the tasks at hand with great understanding and foresight, sometimes seeing further into the future than men. However, Genesis 3:16 reminds us, *"Your desire shall be contrary to your husband, but he shall rule over you."*

Despite their strengths, when faced with challenges or stumbling blocks, women are naturally inclined to turn to men for solutions, protection, and provision. Men, as leaders, are called to address these issues. However, it is dangerous for women to be submissive to ungodly men, and it is even more disastrously complicated for godly women to follow the lead of carnal-minded men.

When women turn to men for answers, men, in turn, must seek God for guidance. Ultimately, both men and women, as a team, must seek and submit to the Lord. This is how God designed it to be, ensuring that His desires for society and humankind are fulfilled.

CHAPTER IX

Realization

Hallelujah! The weight has been lifted from my shoulders. Through divine revelation, God has illuminated the truth to me. This profound realization concerning why the women in my family consistently gravitate towards men who portray an appearance of godliness but lack a genuine relationship with God is a crucial piece of the puzzle in my quest to break the cycle.

Yet, I understand that achieving true liberation from these patterns requires more than mere insight. It demands dedicated effort and unwavering commitment. It is a journey of self-discovery and personal growth, one that I have chosen to embark upon with zeal and determination.

I am fully committed to doing the necessary work, guided by God's revelation and strengthened by His grace. Through introspection and self-improvement, I am determined to overcome these familial patterns and emerge victorious. As I navigate this journey, I am resolved to extend a helping hand to others who are on a similar path, offering support, encouragement, and guidance.

With God's guidance and my steadfast resolve, I am confident that I will not only overcome these cycles but also empower others to do the same. Together, we will break free from the chains of our past and embrace a future filled with hope, redemption, and boundless possibilities.

Realizing that one struggles to manage relationships across various spheres of life can indeed be a significant hurdle when it comes to navigating marriage. Regardless of one's faith or spiritual devotion, the ability to foster healthy relationships with parents, children, siblings, colleagues, and strangers lays the foundation for successful marital relationships.

We've witnessed individuals, revered for their spiritual depth and insight, facing challenges in their marriages. From personal experiences to well-known figures like Juanita Bynum and the late prophetess Kathryn Kuhlman, many others. These instances serve as poignant reminders of the complexities inherent in human relationships.

Marriage demands effective communication, empathy, compromise, and a willingness to navigate conflicts constructively. When one struggles in managing relationships outside of marriage, these same challenges can manifest within the marital bond, potentially leading to discord and ultimately, the breakdown of the union.

Recognizing these difficulties is the first step toward addressing them. Seeking guidance, therapy, or counseling can offer invaluable support in developing the necessary skills and insights to foster healthy relationships, including marriage. It's a journey of growth and self-discovery, one that requires humility, perseverance, and a genuine commitment to personal and relational transformation.

Indeed, while the presence of God is paramount, maintaining successful relationships, including marriage, requires a multifaceted approach. Understanding, wisdom, effective communication, and knowledge are essential components in fostering healthy and lasting connections.

In the context of marriage, traditional gender roles may suggest certain expectations. For women, qualities such as respect, submission, and being a skillful helper are often emphasized. These attributes can contribute to the harmony and strength of the marital bond.

Likewise, men are often viewed as protectors, gentle leaders, and providers within the family unit. Taking responsibility for providing for the family and ensuring the home is orderly are seen as fundamental aspects of their role.

Ultimately, regardless of gender or societal expectations, the key to a successful marriage lies in reverence for God, mutual respect, open communication, shared values, and a willingness to support and uplift one another. By prioritizing these principles, couples can navigate the complexities of married life with grace, understanding, and God's blessings.

How I Know the Cycle Is Broken

God chose to reveal this transformation to me in many ways. I began to notice a significant change in how men behaved toward me. Everywhere I go, I feel protected and supported by them. I no longer feel violated or as though they are after something from me. Instead, they genuinely fulfill their masculine nature toward me in a positive way, without any ill intent.

For example, my neighbor, who had lived next door since I moved in after my divorce, suddenly started cutting my grass for me without asking. This neighbor is married with children, and nothing had changed in my circumstances as a mother with a child. However, something had shifted in the spiritual realm, which then manifested in real life. Suddenly, my neighbor felt the need to protect and support me with no strings attached. Every time the grass needed cutting, he was there, and when I thanked him for his service, he simply replied, *"Just pray for me."* Now, why is he asking me to pray for him while never witnessing me in the act?

This transformation reflects a profound internal shift. When the curse is broken from the inside, it reflects on the outside. My view of men has also changed. I now perceive men as a reflection of God's strength and protection. I feel free to be around them, whereas before, I used to see them as potential heartache.

It is important to note that there are still horrible men around. However, I no longer attract them. The light I carry repels those with ill intentions. The horrible ones seem to flee when they see me, unable to withstand the positive energy and the grace I now exude.

Messages from God's Servants

God has revealed the necessary changes in my life in various ways—through personal dreams, visions, revelations, random messages from strangers, and more. In His goodness, He also chose to confirm these changes through several servants of God in many instances during Godly gatherings.

The scripture in Amos 3:7 says, *"For the Lord God does nothing without revealing his secret to his servants the prophets."* True to this word, He revealed not only to me but to many other servants of God. They delivered powerful prophecies, declaring that "I will achieve what other women in my family could not." This was a clear and undeniable confirmation that God had already brought about the change—the cycle was interrupted; the curse was broken.

It is worth noting that this was my first encounter with Prophet Jules, yet God used him mightily to affirm the breakthrough that had taken place in my life. God is light, and when He moves, His work is unmistakable and undeniable. He will always ensure that His purposes are made known.

Recognizing and Sustaining Change

Just as one needs to meticulously investigate details to uncover familial patterns, it is equally important to pay attention to the details when the cycles are broken. When these cycles are broken, the changes in relationships and behavior—both in yourself and others—become evident. For instance, my brothers now display love and respect, as well as my sisters, and I reciprocate that love and respect. This mutual exchange is a clear sign that the negative cycles have been disrupted.

Setting and maintaining boundaries remains crucial in sustaining these positive changes. Do not violate these boundaries for yourself or others. Recognize and differentiate what constitutes healthy behavior and what does not. It is essential to be mindful of old patterns, as they can resurface if one carelessly undermines the power of generational habits. This is particularly important if you are the one with the grace to break these patterns and stop them from affecting future generations.

Walk firmly and confidently in the victory that God has given you. Continuously seek the Holy Spirit's power to cultivate humility and wisdom. As Psalms 25:9 states, *"He leads the humble in doing right; and teaches the meek His way."* Strive to master communication without resorting to arguments. Cultivate harmony within yourself and with others, and aim to help others flourish as you flourish.

Honor the quality people in your life and around you—your spouse, children, friends, colleagues, spiritual mentors, and brethren. Be a blessing to them as they are to you. This mutual respect and support reinforce the positive changes and prevent old patterns from re-emerging.

By recognizing and nurturing these positive shifts, you ensure that the cycles of the past remain broken, paving the way for a healthier, more fulfilling life for yourself and future generations. Embrace this journey with confidence, humility, and a steadfast commitment to maintaining the newfound harmony and respect in your relationships.

For Women

Recognizing Broken Cycles

When the cycles break, the change is unmistakable and profound. If you are a woman, you will notice a significant shift in how men treat you. Men, in general, will start to protect and support you, regardless of whether they are family members, friends, complete strangers, or your spouse. This shift is a clear indicator that the cycles have been broken.

For instance, look at men in positions of power, such as those in government. They create and enforce specific laws designed to protect women and children. This is a reflection of their intrinsic desire to be helpful and protective. It is inherently rewarding for men to be useful to women without expecting anything in return; this is their God-given nature.

Therefore, if you find yourself being violated, used, disrespected, or abused by men, understand that this behavior is a profound violation of their true nature towards you. Such actions are far from normal and should never be accepted as such. Recognizing this discrepancy is essential in understanding that a fundamental shift needs to occur, either within yourself or in your environment, to break free from these negative cycles.

When these cycles are broken, you will attract positive and respectful interactions with men. They will fulfill their roles as protectors and supporters, not out of obligation, but out of genuine care and respect. This transformation reflects a deep internal change that manifests outwardly, altering your interactions and relationships for the better. You will begin to perceive men as sources of strength and protection, feeling free and secure in their presence, rather than viewing them as potential sources of heartache.

This shift is a testament to the power of breaking free from harmful cycles and embracing a healthier, more respectful dynamic. It is a journey of healing and transformation that, once embarked upon, leads to a life where you are surrounded by men who honor their true nature and, in turn, help you thrive.

The earlier women develop virtues such as submission, respect, resourcefulness, companionship, and spirituality, the better they can attract the right men into their lives. Men are leaders—let them lead. They were created to lead. Women were created to help them lead. This means women do not have to carry the burdens of leadership on our shoulders. We can lead from our place of submission and still be effective.

Clarification: The word "submission" does not imply being enslaved or regarded as inferior; rather, it means embracing and allowing your God-given nature and identity to radiate. While women can indeed be powerful leaders, our leadership is distinct from that of men. Women's leadership stems from a place of nurturing and gentleness, creating an environment where others feel supported and valued. In contrast, men's leadership is often characterized by a more stern and straightforward approach.

It is crucial to understand that women who attempt to lead with masculine energy may encounter difficulties, as men may be less inclined to cooperate with female leaders exhibiting these traits. Each gender brings unique strengths and perspectives to leadership, and it is essential to honor and embrace these differences. Recognizing and respecting these complementary qualities enables a more harmonious and effective leadership dynamic, where both men and women can thrive and contribute meaningfully.

Queen Elizabeth II

Let's talk about an important figure who led the British kingdom for decades: Queen Elizabeth II. By taking the time to listen to her speeches to the nations, we can uncover her natural strength and influence. Queen Elizabeth II's speeches were characterized by her demure demeanor, poised presence, and genuine care for her people, allowing her feminine energy to shine through.

Her leadership was marked by immense power and grace, earning her the admiration of people around the world. She possessed an astute understanding of when to defend herself and her kingdom. In meetings with world leaders, if she ever felt offended by a comment, she deftly used humor to address the situation and assert her authority. This combination of strength, poise, and wit enabled her to govern effectively and command respect on the global stage. Queen Elizabeth II's reign exemplified how feminine energy, when embraced, can lead to powerful and admired leadership.

For Men

Recognizing Broken Cycles

Men, if you want to know if negative cycles and patterns have been broken, pay attention to how women show respect to you. Whether it is your mother, sisters, cousins, or a complete stranger, respect is essential. It is not natural for you to constantly deal with women who are disrespectful and condescending. It is hard to be in your element if you are not revered and honored. When women treat you with respect, it becomes easier to fulfill your role.

Respect is a value that must be cultivated from the inside out. It begins within yourself and naturally extends to those closest to you—your mother, spouse, sisters, and then to friends and acquaintances. When respect is present in your close relationships, it empowers you to fully embrace the roles God intended for you: protector, provider, leader, and more.

Men, it is paramount to cultivate your relationship with God the Father. As leaders, you will inevitably face challenges that only the head of the Church, Jesus Christ, can help you navigate. The closer you are to God and the more you revere Him, the safer and more effective you will be in your mission. As 1 Corinthians 11:3 emphasizes, *"But I want you to understand that the head of every man is Christ, the head of a wife is her husband, and the head of Christ is God."*

Consider Sarah, who referred to Abraham as her lord, as mentioned in 1 Peter 3:6: *"As Sarah obeyed Abraham, calling him lord. You are her children, if you do good and do not fear anything that is frightening."* Sarah's deep respect for Abraham wasn't born out of vanity or obligation; it stemmed from Abraham's leadership and reverence for God. Her respect was a response to the safety, provision, and protection that Abraham consistently provided for her.

True respect in a relationship is earned through actions that reflect God's love and care. It allows both individuals to flourish in their God-given roles, creating an environment where respect is mutual and deeply rooted in faith and love.

Insights

The respect that men inherently crave goes beyond the universal respect we offer each other as human beings. It is a deeper, more profound respect, which the Bible often refers to as submissiveness. This kind of respect is not merely about acknowledging someone's humanity; it is about honoring the unique roles and responsibilities that men are called to fulfill.

As stated in 1 Timothy 2:11: *"Let a woman learn quietly with all submissiveness."* This passage speaks to the importance of a deeper respect rooted in understanding and reverence for the order God has established. Submissiveness, in this context, is not about subservience but about recognizing and supporting the God-given roles that men and women have in their relationships.

This deeper respect fosters an environment where men can thrive in their roles as protectors, providers, and leaders. It is through this mutual understanding and respect that both men and women can fulfill their God-given purposes, creating a harmonious and balanced relationship.

Men, please know it is important for us women to have responsible and God-fearing men around us. It makes us feel safer and more productive in our roles. Therefore, cultivate your manhood and pay attention to repetitive issues in your relationships with women and with people in general. Respect is foundational to healthy, fulfilling relationships and to your ability to fully embrace your God-given roles.

In the book of Genesis, women were not the first gift awarded to Adam in the Garden of Eden; instead, his responsibilities came first. On the sixth day, when God created Adam, his duties were already awaiting him—caring for and naming the animals and tending to the earth. It was not until later, when God recognized that Adam needed help, that He created Eve. As Genesis 2:18 states, *"Then the LORD God said, 'It is not good that the man should be alone; I will make him a helper fit for him.'"*

This order is significant: it suggests that men must first identify and commit to their mission and responsibilities before bringing women into their lives to form a team.

Men, even when women are in positions of leadership, you can still lead by understanding your mission and identity. God does not make mistakes in His intentions for humanity. While it is true that women can often do everything men can do—and sometimes even better—there's an inherent dynamic where women naturally look to men for solutions to unresolved challenges in every facet of life. As men, your role is to seek answers from God, and together, both men and women must ultimately rely on God as the source of everything.

Finally

Beloved, I understand that change is rarely easy, but it is always worth the effort. When we are called to break generational cycles or transform challenging situations, it requires an unwavering determination to move forward. It is tempting to ignore pain, hoping it will vanish on its own, but we must ask ourselves: how far can we truly go by avoiding the truth? Real progress is made by renewing our strength in the Spirit of God, embracing the life He has planned for us.

No matter the area in which you are called to bring freedom—whether it's for yourself, your family, a community, or a nation—remember that if you are the one who recognizes the problem, you are also the one equipped to overcome it. The grace of God is more than sufficient. Stay focused, vigilant, and steadfast. The victory has already been secured, and the cycles are broken.

"Do not be afraid. Stand still and see the salvation of the Lord, which He will accomplish for you today. For the Egyptians whom you see today, you shall see again no more forever." (Exodus 14:13)

Conclusion

Breaking the chains of dysfunction and generational patterns requires more than just the presence of God, though His presence is undoubtedly the most crucial element. To truly overcome these chains, we also need understanding, wisdom, communication, and knowledge. In my own life, I was initially unaware of the significance of my curiosity about my family's history and stories. Every detail captivated me, though I did not fully understand why. It was only through this exploration that I began to see the patterns—like attracting the same type of men or being labeled as the black sheep—that had subtly but powerfully influenced my path, setting the stage for me to fall into the same traps that ensnared those before me.

Understanding that a pattern initiated in one generation can bind future generations to the same struggles is crucial. In my family, these patterns began long before me, trickling down through my aunts, sisters, and other women related to me. It wast not until this pattern was revealed to me that I realized it needed to be broken. Nevertheless, breaking a generational cycle is not a simple task. When an altar is raised in darkness, it initiates a spiritual battle, a fight that requires strength, focus, and divine intervention to overcome.

Just as it was perilous for me, it may be difficult for you to persevere as well. The journey of breaking curses and cycles is often filled with challenges and obstacles. However, if you are the one chosen to break these curses, know that you are equipped to do so. *"We are more than conquerors"* (Romans 8:37). This victory can only be achieved through God's grace. The grace of God is not only the source of our strength but also the key to the effectiveness of our efforts in bringing down those spiritual Jerichos in our lives.

Furthermore, as we navigate these challenges, it is vital to understand and embrace our God-given roles. Men and women were created to complement each other. A woman is called to be respectful, submissive, and a skillful helpmate. A man, in turn, is called to be a protector, a gentle leader, and a provider. These roles are not just important in the context of marriage only but are essential in every aspect of life. Recognizing and living out these roles is integral to breaking chains and establishing a healthy, God-centered life.

Knowing your identity in Christ brings confidence and clarity, enabling you to align yourself with the purpose and plan God has for you. When you understand who you are in Christ, you can face the challenges of breaking cycles with the assurance that you are not alone, and that victory is within your reach.

Breaking generational patterns and chains is not an easy journey, but it is a vital one. It requires a deep commitment to understanding the roots of these cycles, as well as a willingness to confront and address them with perseverance. Equally important is the application of basic biblical principles regarding God's design for humankind. However, with God's grace, wisdom, and strength, it is possible to break free from these chains, paving the way for

future generations to live in the freedom and fullness of
God's blessings.

Let's Pray

Father God, You deserve all the praises and adoration, for there is no one like You. Please hear me and the reader as we unite in Your name. Your word says, *"For when two or three are gathered together in Your name, You are in the midst of them"* (Matthew 18:20). First, we ask for Your forgiveness for our trespasses and for those who have trespassed against us. We know that there is no stain from sin and iniquity that Your blood cannot wash away. Thank You for Your sacrifice on Calvary.

Father God, I pray that as the reader finishes this book, You reveal to them any minor details of negative generational patterns. Help them uncover the root causes of these cycles and give them the power and wisdom to break them. Work on their hearts now.

Thank You, Holy Spirit, for Your guidance as You light up our way. You are the best teacher there ever is. Please help anyone who reads this book to discover the hindrances on their paths and the patterns in their lives that have seemed subtle yet have caused destruction. I ask You, Father, as I agree with them in this prayer, to open their minds and understanding so they can recognize unhealthy patterns and curses within their families. There are no obstacles You cannot remove; no mountains You cannot move. Right now, by the power of the Holy Spirit, I break every chain, I bring down every pattern that appears as a mountain to them. I declare that their eyes are open to realize the generational patterns that have plagued their families.

Please, Father, give them the wisdom and grace to break these curses and chains once and for all. Let them experience the freedom that only You can grant to Your children. I declare it is done in Jesus's name.

Thank You, ABBA.

Amen.

A Prayer of Salvation

Lord Jesus, I believe that You are the Son of God. I believe that You died, were resurrected, and are now seated at the right hand of the Father, pleading my case. I believe Your blood was shed on Calvary for the forgiveness of my sins and the salvation of my soul. Today, right here, right now, I repent of my sins and accept You as my Lord and Savior. Thank You for accepting me as Your child from this day forward.

Amen.

If you say this prayer wholeheartedly, you are saved. Next, find a church led by Christ where you can be planted for continuous Bible instruction and grow in faith.